Lola and Lupe's House

Written by Megan Borgert-Spaniol

Illustrated by Lisa Hunt

GRL Consultants, Diane Craig and Monica Marx, Certified Literacy Specialists

Lerner Publications ◆ Minneapolis

Note from a GRL Consultant
This Pull Ahead leveled book has been carefully designed for beginning readers. A team of guided reading literacy experts has reviewed and leveled the book to ensure readers pull ahead and experience success.

Lerner Publications Company
An imprint of Lerner Publishing Group, Inc.
241 First Avenue North
Minneapolis, MN 55401 USA

For reading levels and more information, look up this title at www.lernerbooks.com.

Main body text set in Mikado 24/41
Typeface provided by Hannes von Doehren.

The images in this book are used with the permission of: Lisa Hunt

Library of Congress Cataloging-in-Publication Data

Names: Borgert-Spaniol, Megan, 1989- author. | Hunt, Lisa (Lisa Jane), 1973– illustrator.
Title: Lola and Lupe's house / Megan Borgert-Spaniol ; illustrated by Lisa Hunt.
Description: Minneapolis, MN : Lerner Publications, [2022] | Series: Helpful habits. Pull ahead readers. People smarts. Fiction | Includes index. | Audience: Ages 4–7. | Audience: Grades K–1. | Summary: "Should Lola and Lupe's house be yellow or green? At first they can't agree, so they have to work together to find a compromise. Pairs with the nonfiction title Working with Others"— Provided by publisher.
Identifiers: LCCN 2020014691 (print) | LCCN 2020014692 (ebook) | ISBN 9781728403571 (library binding) | ISBN 9781728423289 (paperback) | ISBN 9781728418339 (ebook)
Subjects: LCSH: Readers (Primary) | Cooperativeness—Juvenile fiction.
Classification: LCC PE1119 .B6976 2020 (print) | LCC PE1119 (ebook) | DDC 428.6/2—dc23

LC record available at https://lccn.loc.gov/2020014691
LC ebook record available at https://lccn.loc.gov/2020014692

Manufactured in the United States of America
2-1010757-48895-3/12/2024

Table of Contents

Lola and Lupe's House

Lola and Lupe made a house.

“Let’s paint it green,”
Lola said.

“Let’s paint it yellow,”
Lupe said.

“Green!”
Lola said.

“Yellow!”
Lupe said.

Lola looked at the house.

Lola and Lupe painted the house.